SPRING FORWARD, FALL BACK IN LOVE

Carol Preflatish

PUBLISHER
PreComm Communications

Cover Artist: Dawne Dominique
Front Cover Art Layout: DusktilDawn Designs
Back Cover Design: Mysti Parker

Dedication

To Mom, who I used to tease about
reading smutty books.

Chapter One

Grace Taylor exited her car at the small hotel in Summit, Colorado. Her hometown had grown so much since she left ten years ago after high school. She never thought she would return, but here she was.

After checking in at the hotel, she drove outside of town to the Buck Creek Ranch and Stables. When she walked into the office, she immediately recognized the man behind the counter.

"Mr. Watkins?" she asked.

"Yes. Can I help you?" He had an inquisitive look on his face as if trying to figure out who she was. "Grace? Grace Caldwell?"

"That's me, except it's Taylor now."

"Oh my gosh. Come here and let me give you a hug." He came around the counter and did just that. "I don't think I've seen you since your high school graduation."

"That's right. This is my first trip back."

"How are your parents? You all moved Colorado Springs, right?"

"Yes. Dad got a job there and I attended the university. They're still there and doing well."

"That's good to hear. What brings you back?"

"My company is hosting a retreat for some of the employees. My co-workers know that I used to ride horses in competition, but that's been so long ago that I thought I would come for a refresher course."

"You know as well as I do that you never forget how to ride. There's something else." He crooked his head waiting for an answer.

"The last time I rode was my first year in college and I got thrown. I haven't been back on since."

"Well, we'll fix you right up. When do you want to start?"

"How about tomorrow morning?"

"Be here by ten and I'll have a horse and instructor waiting for you."

"That would be great."

"I'll tell Cindy you're in town too, if you don't mind."

"Is she still around?"

"She went to college but moved back about five years ago. She practically runs the Blue Spruce Hotel."

"Really? That's where I'm staying. I'll make sure to look her up."

"You two were practically inseparable when you were kids."

"I know. I can't wait to see her. Is her last name still Watkins?"

"Yeah, her mom and I keep hoping she'll marry and give us some grandkids, but that hasn't happened yet. How about you?"

"Me, kids? No, I actually just divorced a few months ago."

"I'm sorry to hear that, but you keep looking. You never know when the right person will show up."

"I suppose. I'll see you in the morning."

Watkins gave her wave goodbye and she headed outside to her car. She looked around the ranch remembering how it used to look. Several men stood next to the stable and then walked inside. With the sun so bright, she had difficulty seeing. *Was that? No, it couldn't have been.*

"That couldn't have been Andy. He wanted out of this town as much as I did back then," she said aloud. She got in her car and drove back to the hotel. When she walked into the lobby, she heard someone call her name.

"Grace, wait."

She turned around to see Cindy Watkins hurrying to catch up to her. The two ladies hugged. "It's so good to see you. I just left your dad."

"I know. He called to tell me you were in town and staying here." Cindy held up her cell phone.

Grace chuckled. "I forgot how fast news travels around here. You look wonderful and your dad said you run the hotel."

Now it was Cindy's turn to laugh. "Not exactly. Dad gets a little carried away when he talks about me. I'm the Events Coordinator for the conferences held here at the hotel. I set up the entertainment, a concert every once in a while, but mostly I work with corporations for their conferences."

"I guess you set up the retreat for my company next weekend."

"Probably so. What's the company?"

"The Myers Corporation out of Denver."

"Yes, that would be me. As I recall, there's a trail ride scheduled."

"And, that's why I'm here now. I need to brush up on my riding skills."

"You? You were a champion rider back in school. One whole wall of your room was covered with ribbons and trophies."

"It's a long story, but I haven't ridden since my first year of college."

Cindy's cell phone began to buzz. She looked at it and then at Grace. "I've got to go, but I'd love to catch up. Would you like to meet for dinner tonight?"

"I'm afraid I have a conference call this evening for work. Could we make it tomorrow night?"

"Sure, that would work better for me anyway. How about seven o'clock in the hotel's restaurant?"

"Perfect."

"I'll make the reservation. See you then." Cindy rushed off, and Grace took the elevator to her room.

The next morning, Grace walked into the office at Buck Creek Ranch. This time, instead of Mr. Watkins, a young lady stood behind the counter. "Can I help you?"

"Yes. I'm Grace Taylor and I have a riding lesson scheduled at ten."

The lady typed something on the computer. "We have you listed right here. How many lessons will you be taking?"

"I'd like to try it for three days."

"Great." She typed more on the computer. "I'll need a credit card and you know these are non-refundable lessons."

"I understand."

The girl swiped the credit card and then gave Grace the slip to sign, as well as a couple release forms. "Thanks you. If you'll have a seat on the porch, I'll send the trail guide out to get you."

Grace walked out and sat down in one of the wooden rocking chairs. The spring day couldn't have been better for riding—sunny and cool with a light breeze. She remembered days like this when she, Cindy and Andy used to clean the stables at the Carver's ranch down the road. She had the best memories from working there.

"Miss Taylor?" a male voice called from the end of the porch.

She rose from the chair and turned to find Andy Granger waiting for her. "Andy?" She rose from the chair and turned to find Andy Granger waiting for her. Her high school boyfriend was the last person she had hoped to run into, but now that he was in front of her, she felt her knees go a little weak. He took off his cowboy hat and wiped the sweat from his brow with his sleeve. His clingy shirt and tight jeans sent her heart into palpitations. She had to take a deep breath to calm herself.

He stepped upon the porch. "Gracie, what are you doing here?"

"I'm here for riding lessons."

"I'm your trail guide."

"No! No way am I going out on a ride with you. Get me another guide," she demanded.

"I'm the only one available."

Grace turned and went back into the main office followed by Andy. With the young lady gone, Mr. Watkins now stood behind the counter.

"Hello, Grace. Ready for your ride?" He glanced at Andy.

"Mr. Watkins, are there any other guides available, other than Andy?"

"What's wrong with Andy?"

"Remember, he and I used to date in high school and then we

broke up?"

"But, that was eight years ago. Don't you think you've both put your past behind you?"

"I would really prefer a different guide."

Mr. Watkins scratched his head. "Well, honey, I'm really sorry, but all the other guides are already out for the day."

Grace looked at Andy.

"It's me or nothing," he said.

"Fine!" She stomped out of the building, her boots clacking on the hardwood floor as she did.

Andy followed her out. "Gracie, wait." He grabbed her arm.

"Don't call me that." She jerked her arm out of his grasp.

"I always called you that."

"Not any more. That was a long time ago. Let's just stick to Grace."

"Whatever you want."

She turned and started toward the barn.

"Will you wait? I want to talk to you."

She stopped and put her hands on her hips. "What?"

"Why do you need riding lessons? You used to be one of the best riders around."

"I'm getting tired of explaining that. During my first year of college, I was riding with some friends and I got thrown when my horse stepped in a prairie dog hole. I hit my head resulting in a concussion, but even worse, my horse broke her leg and we had to put Oreo down. I wasn't paying attention. It was all my fault." A tear escaped the corner of her eye and trailed down her cheek before she wiped it away.

"Oreo? The horse you grew up with?"

"Yes."

"I'm sorry. I know how much you love that horse."

"I haven't ridden since."

"It wasn't your fault. Prairie dog holes are hard to see. It could happen to anyone."

"Can we get started?" She wiped her eyes and headed toward the barn,

Andy caught up and walked in silence along side of her. When they entered the barn, she stopped when she saw the two horses saddled and waiting for them.

"Is that Ricochet?" She walked over to the black horse and it immediately started nuzzling her.

"He remembers you," Andy said. "I don't usually ride him here at work, but I thought I was teaching a beginner today and it would be an easy ride for him."

"An easy ride is what I want."

"You'll be riding Rosebud. She's about as gentle as they come."

Grace walked over to the chestnut colored horse. "Hi girl, I'm Grace." The horse dipped her head as if to say hi back.

Andy got on Ricochet and turned to Grace. "I don't know how much instruction you need, so you'll have to let me know when you need help."

"I will." She grabbed the horn of the saddle, but hesitated

before mounting the horse, just staring at the saddle.

"Grace, are you okay?"

His voice startled her. "Yes, I just needed a minute." She mounted the horse and let out a sigh of relief.

"We're going to take the low land trail. It's a mile loop, level, and a pretty easy ride."

"That sounds like a good start."

Through a gate and along a row of fencing and she was off on her first ride in ten years.

"Can I ask you a question," Andy inquired.

"You can ask, but I might not answer."

"Fair enough. Your name on the registration form said Taylor. Are you married?"

Since they had known each other for a long time, Grace decided it was a fair question. "I was. My divorce was recently final. I probably should have changed my name back, but with work and all, it was just easier to keep his name."

"I'm sorry to hear about the divorce."

"Oh, I'm not. He was a jerk. I divorced him. He cheated on me," she admitted.

"I can't imagine anyone cheating on you."

"Can we not talk about this?"

"Sure. Sorry."

They rode a few more yards down the trail. "It's so beautiful here. I never thought I would miss this place, but coming back I think I'm beginning to."

"Where do you live now?" he asked.

"In Denver."

"A city girl now, eh?"

"Maybe a little, but I think I'm feeling the country coming back."

The trail now led them out into a large field that Grace knew contained prairie dog holes. She stopped her horse.

"Why are you stopping?"

"I don't want her stepping in a hole."

"You can tell by the worn grass where the trail is, so there shouldn't be any to step in. I'll go in front and keep an eye out."

"Okay."

They made it through the field with no problems and the trail now led them along the base of a mountain. She watched Andy ahead of her as they maneuvered around trees and boulders. She noticed how he hadn't changed much since high school. Older now, but just as handsome. He had definitely stayed in shape over the years. Working on a ranch will keep you that way, she figured.

One thing she didn't notice was whether he wore a wedding ring. She chastised herself for the thought. He was the last person she needed to become interested in.

An hour later, they came to a shelter house with a picnic table and a stream flowing by. "This is the halfway point. We can take a break here," he suggested, dismounting from his horse.

Grace got down from her horse, feeling a little stiff. "I have a feeling I may not be able to move tomorrow."

"After this short trip?"

"I haven't used these muscles in ten years, remember?"

Andy laughed. "I suppose you're right."

He opened one of his saddlebags and got out two bottles of water and a couple small plastic zipper bags. "Here, some water and something to snack on."

When he handed her the water, she looked at his hand. No wedding ring and no tan line indicating one he wasn't wearing.

"Thanks." She took the water and he placed one of the bags on the table. "What's in the other bag?"

"Carrots for the horses."

"Can I give it to them?" she asked.

"Sure." He handed her the bag.

She walked over to where the horses were getting a drink from the water trough by the stream.

"Here you go, Ricochet. A little treat for you and Rosebud." She held her hand out flat with a few carrots on her palm. She took turns letting the horses eat.

"How long are you here for, Grace?"

"Three days for lessons and then back next weekend for my company retreat and ride."

"Is Buck Creek doing your trail ride?"

"No, Blue Spruce Hotel is handing the whole retreat." With no more carrots left, she walked back over to join him at the table.

"I guess Cindy is handling things over there then."

"Yes. I saw her yesterday and she said he set up the whole thing. We're having dinner together tonight at the hotel."

"I'm sure she'll catch you up on the old gang. Who's married to who and who's divorced from who, and who's sleeping with who."

"It sounds like things don't change much."

"No, not much. If you're finished, we probably should be heading back to the ranch."

"I'm ready." She took one last drink of water and handed the bottle and empty carrot bag back to Andy, and he stowed it back in his saddlebag.

Back on the horses and on the trail, Grace paid closer attention to the mountains in front of them. Even with the spring warming in the valley, the winter snows were still in the mountains. "Do you think we could take a trip on a mountain trail on the last day?" she asked.

"If you think you'll be up to that, I don't see why not. You seem to be getting comfortable again in the saddle."

"We'll see how tomorrow goes first."

"I think I'll take you on a moderate trail tomorrow, with a little more grade to it, especially if you want to go on a mountain trail the next day."

"Okay." She did feel more comfortable than when she first got on the horse. She hated to admit it to herself, but it helped having Andy as her guide.

When they reached the field, she didn't hesitate this time. In fact, she rode next to Andy instead of following behind him. She still kept a close eye out for holes though.

Around the bend and they reached the fencerow, the last stretch of the ride.

"Feel like taking it a little faster to the finish?" he asked.

"Maybe just an easy gallop, but not full speed."

"Let's go." He gave Ricochet a little kick with his heels and off he went.

"Andy, I said easy gallop," she called after him. Kicking her heels she took off after him.

* * * *

"Grace, over here." Cindy Watkins waved at Grace as she came into the restaurant.

"Hi, Cindy. I thought I was going to be so late and you'd be gone." Grace sat down, winded.

"You're not so late. Did you have a busy day?"

"I did." The waitress came to the table to take Grace's drink order. "I'll have a Cosmopolitan, please." With her order, the waitress left. "I had my riding lesson this morning and then had some work to do in my room before coming here."

"You did have a big day. How was your lesson? Is everything coming back?"

Grace laughed. "More things came back than I hoped. Did you know that Andy was a trail guide at Buck Creek Stables?"

"Yes, I did. He works for dad. I wish I had thought of that to warn you. Sorry."

"I nearly went into shock when he stepped on the porch!" I had hoped I wouldn't run into him while here. I even asked your dad if anyone else was available but there wasn't." She shook her head. "I don't know how I'm going to make it through two more rides with him."

"High school was so long ago and you're both adults now. I assume you've moved on since your last name is Taylor now."

"I divorced a few months ago and how did you know that?"

"I checked your hotel reservation and gave you a discount. You were the only Grace registered, so I figured it must have been you."

"You gave me a discount? Thanks. That was so nice." She reached across the table and gave Cindy a hug.

"You're welcome. It's only ten percent, but I like to do that with friends. Do you have any kids? That's usually why women don't change their name after a divorce."

"No, no kids. I thought about changing it back, but my business contacts know me by Taylor, it was just easier to keep it for work. Your dad told me that you haven't married. Aren't there plenty of eligible bachelors around here to choose from?"

"There are and contrary to what my dad says, I have my share of dates. Right now, I want to secure my career for the future before I concentrate on a husband and family."

"I know. I got married too young and too fast. I was right out of college and had started my new job. We thought we were in love, but honestly we should have just lived together for a while. It lasted a little over three years."

"I'm sorry to hear that. I want a family, but just not yet."

"Richard wanted a family too, but he wanted me to be a stay at home mom. I spent too much money and time on a college degree to throw that away. I wanted a career in addition to being a mom."

"Well, good for you."

After their dinner, Grace decided to call it a night and stood. "This has been so much fun, Cindy. I've really missed talking with you."

"If you don't have to go right back to your room, there's a bar down the street where a lot of the locals hang out. We could drop in for a few drinks," Cindy suggested.

She thought only momentarily about the work she needed to do and the emails that needed answered before making her decision. "That sounds like fun. I'm in."

Grace got her credit card out, but Cindy stopped her. "Put that away. This dinner is on me."

"I couldn't let you do that. It's too much."

"You buy us a few rounds at the bar and we'll call it even."

"Deal."

Cindy told the waitress to put the bill on her account and the ladies left the hotel, walking down the street and across a parking lot to the Silver Bullet Saloon.

Although not crowded, the establishment seemed to be pretty busy for a Monday night. Cindy found them a table near the bar and once Grace's eyes adjusted to the dim lighting, she could see a stage across the room from them, a long bar close to them, lots of tables—most of them with people seated, and a large dance floor with several couples dancing to the piped in music.

"This is nice. As I remember, this used to be a hardware store," Grace said.

"You're right. Once the big discount store came in outside of town, the hardware store closed."

A young man wearing tight jeans and a cowboy shirt and hat came up to their table. "Hi Cindy. How are you this evening?"

"I'm fine, Bobby. How are you?"

"I'm finer than frog hair. What can I get you ladies to drink tonight?"

"I think I'd like a Mohito," Cindy said.

"I'll take a rum and Coke," Grace added.

"Great. I'll get 'em right out to you," Bobby said.

"Cindy, why did you decide to stay here in Summit rather than get away?"

"I did get away for a while. Like you, I went to college, but it was in Fort Collins and I studied Hospitality Services. My plan was to work at one of the big hotels in Vail or Aspen after I graduated."

"Why didn't you do that?"

"I don't know. I guess I liked my hometown too much to leave."

"Here you go, ladies. One Mohito and one rum and Coke."

"Thanks, Bobby."

"Will you be running a tab tonight, or are you just having one drink tonight?"

Cindy looked at Grace, who said, "We'll be running a tab. It's on me."

"Fantastic," he said. "Cindy, I don't think I know your friend here."

"Bobby, this is Grace Taylor, my best friend from high school. Grace, this is Bobby, one of the best waiters in town and also a damn good chef. I keep trying to talk him into coming to work at the Blue Spruce, but he won't leave the Buck Creek Ranch."

"Ah Cindy, you know I don't want to cook for those uppity people over there." He looked at Grace and took her hand, kissing it gently. "It's a pleasure meeting you."

"Careful, Bobby. Grace is one of those uppity people staying at the hotel."

Shock spread across his face. "I'm sorry, ma'am. I didn't mean to insinuate that you were a snob or anything."

Grace laughed. "I forgive you."

"Anything else you need, you just give ol' Bobby a shout." He gave Grace a smile as he walked away.

"He was flirting with me," Grace said.

"Don't get your hopes up. He was playing for a big tip. Bobby's gay."

Both ladies laughed at his theatrics. "He's pretty good."

"The real reason he won't leave Buck Creek is because of all the cowboys that work over there."

"He and I have something in common then. I kind of like cowboys too."

"Oh no," Cindy groaned. "Grace, we shouldn't have come here. I'm so sorry."

"Sorry? Why?"

"Don't turn around, but Andy just walked in."

Grace didn't move. "Maybe he won't see me."

"No, he already has and he's walking over here."

"Hi Cindy," he said when he approached their table.

"Hi, Andy. How are you?"

"I'm doing just fine. How's work at the hotel?"

"Oh, we're busy as always."

"Hello, Grace."

She looked up at him and felt her heart skip a beat. He wore tight boot-cut jeans, blue plaid flannel shirt, and gray cowboy hat. She always liked men in cowboy hats. "Hello." She looked away. She had to resist.

"How do you feel after your ride this morning?"

"I feel fine."

He let out a little laugh. "Just wait until morning. That's when it will hit you."

"I'm not out of shape. I think I can handle an hour of horseback riding without becoming an invalid," she snapped.

"Hey, Andy! How ya doing, my man?" Another guy in jeans and cowboy hat walked up and slapped Andy on the back.

"Chuck," Cindy said. "Don't act like such a child."

"Are we a little jealous that I didn't greet my little lady first?" He leaned down and gave her a kiss on the cheek.

"Yeah, that's it." Sarcasm.

"I'm fine, Chuck," Andy said. "Ladies, it was nice talking to you." He started to walk away.

"Wait a minute. Join us," Chuck said, sitting down next to Cindy.

He looked at Grace. "No, I better not." He turned and walked over to the bar.

"You can really be a jerk sometimes, do you know that?" Cindy said to Chuck.

"What?" he asked.

"Chuck, this is Grace Taylor, an old high school friend of mine. Grace, this is Chuck Payne, someone I spend a lot of time with."

"Oh Cindy, just call me your boyfriend and get it over with. It's nice to meet your Grace."

"Nice to meet you too."

"What's with the remark about being a jerk?" he asked Cindy.

"Grace didn't want Andy sitting with us. They used to date."

"How was I supposed to know that?"

"It's okay, really," Grace broke in.

He looked at Grace. "I'm sorry."

"No harm, no foul."

Chuck held his arm up and gave a little wave to Bobby to bring him a drink.

"So Grace, since I've not met you before, I assume you no longer live here?"

"I live in Denver now."

"What do you do for a living?"

"I'm a marketing consultant for the Myers Corporation. What do you do here in Summit?"

"I'm the Restaurant Manager at the Blue Spruce."

"Oh, now I understand why Cindy said something about Bobby coming to work there."

"Chuck is an excellent chef himself, but prefers the management side of things right now," Cindy said.

"I hope you will come to the restaurant while you're in town."

"I already have," she replied. "We ate there this evening. Very good food."

"Thank you."

"Grace is staying at the hotel for a few days and will be back over the weekend for a company retreat."

"That's wonderful. I'll see to it that you get a discount on all of your meals there," Chuck said.

"You don't have to do that."

"No, I insist. You're a friend and I always treat my friends."

"Here you go, Chuck." Bobby sat a long-neck bottle on the table. "You wanted your usual beer, right?"

"Yes, I did. Run a tab and put these lovely ladies' drinks on it."

"Will do," Bobby said and left.

Someone started the jukebox up and music filled the room. Several couples got up to dance.

"Would you like to dance, sweetie?" Chuck asked Cindy.

"I'd hate to leave Grace alone at the table."

"No, you go ahead. I don't mind."

Chuck stood and took Cindy by the hand and led her to the dance floor.

No sooner had they left than Andy sat down with Grace. "Would you like to dance?"

"I don't think so," she answered.

"What's wrong, Gracie?"

"I don't know what you mean."

"Ever since this morning, I've tried to be nice, be just friends and you've done your best to keep me at a distance. Why?"

"You're imagining things." She tried not to keep eye contact with him; instead she watched the dancers on the floor.

"Then dance with me. Just friends dancing."

If she said no, he would know she really was trying to avoid him. But, to be that close to him again; she wasn't sure that was a good idea either. "Okay, one dance."

"Great."

As she stood up, the song that had been playing ended and a slower song started. Andy took her hand and guided her to the dance floor. He placed his hand on her lower back and she was surprised that he kept space between them, and a little disappointed too.

"How does it feel to be back in Summit?" he asked.

"All right, I guess. Things around here have changed so much in the few years I've been gone."

"Changed for the better. The town's practically grown into a city now with all the hotels and ranches. There's one company that's going to build a ski resort next summer for the winter season."

"Skiing?" She chuckled.

"I know what you're thinking."

"What's that?"

"You're remembering when you, me, Cindy, and Dan borrowed some skis from Mr. Poole and went to the high country."

"Borrowed? I don't recall us asking."

"We returned them."

"We did, but not in the same condition."

Andy laughed. "It's a wonder we didn't break our necks trying to ski on that mountain."

"We were stupid kids back then. Did you ever learn to ski?"

"You know, I did. I went to Vail with some friends a couple years later and I learned. I'm pretty good at it too."

"You always could do things like that well."

"How about you? Did you learn?"

"Yes. My ex-husband taught me on a trip to Aspen right after we were married. Not exactly a trip I want to remember though." She suddenly realized that while dancing, they had both moved closer together. "I think I'd like to sit down now," she said reluctantly after the song ended.

She stepped away and they went back to the table where Cindy and Chuck were seated.

"You two looked good out there together," Chuck said.

Neither Grace or Andy replied.

"I'm going to have to get home," Cindy said. "I have to be at the office early in the morning. Grace, would you like me to walk back to the hotel with you?"

Before Grace could answer, Andy jumped in. "I'd be glad to walk her back."

"Great, that way I can drive Cindy home," Chuck added.

"Is that okay, Grace?" Cindy asked.

"Sure, I'm a big girl. I think I can handle him."

The group laughed.

"I'll give you a call tomorrow afternoon. You have one more night at the hotel right?" Cindy asked.

"Yes, then I'll be back for the weekend with my co-workers."

"It was nice meeting you, Grace," Chuck said. "I hope you'll come visit here more often. I'd like to hear some of your stories of growing up with my little lady here." He wrapped his arm around Cindy and pulled her closer.

"It was nice meeting you too, but I'm not sure if I'll be back again after this weekend, or not."

Grace reached into her purse and took out her wallet.

"No, the tab is on me tonight," Chuck said.

"Thank you. That's nice. If there's a next time, it'll be on me."

Cindy and Chuck left hand in hand, leaving Grace and Andy standing there.

"I suppose we should go, if you want to get back to the hotel," he said.

"Yes, I do. I have a few things I need to finish for work and email in tonight."

They started out the door. "You're working while you're here?"

"Yes. It's the only way I could get off to come here. My boss thinks I'm at some family function. I wasn't about to let them know I came here to bush up on my riding skills."

Out on the street, the full moon reflected off of the snow-covered mountains outside of town.

"I'm always amazed at how beautiful the mountains look in

the moonlight. You don't get that kind of view in Denver," Grace said, gazing at the sky.

"I never thought of you as a city girl."

"I've changed over the years. I love the city now."

"You don't miss living here?"

"No, not at all."

They continued walking. With the cool spring temperature, she shivered.

"Here, take my jacket," he offered.

"No, I don't need that."

"We still have a couple blocks to walk, you take it."

She obliged and he helped her on with the jacket. "Thanks."

They continued on their walk.

"Chuck doesn't seem like the type I thought Cindy would end up with," Grace said.

"You know, she went off to college like you, but came back here to work and has a great life with Chuck now. I'm sure they'll get married and have a family soon."

" It's good to know that kind of thing works for some people."

They reached her hotel and Andy opened the door for her. Both walked inside. "Thanks for walking me back, but I think I can make it to my room myself."

"Oh, sure. I'll see you around ten in the morning for your next ride, I guess."

"I'll be there." She turned and headed toward the elevators and suddenly realized she still had his jacket on. "Great," she mumbled to herself and turned to find that Andy had already walked out of the lobby. "I'll take it to him tomorrow." Still wearing the jacket, she could smell the scent of his aftershave on it. She stepped onto the elevator and went to her room.

Chapter Two

Grace's alarm sounded on her cell phone the next morning and she reached over to turn it off. "Ouch!"

She sat up on the side of the bed and it felt as though every muscle in her body ached. "Maybe I'm not in as good a shape as I thought."

Slowly, she stood and rubbed her back as she sauntered to the bathroom where she turned the shower water on as hot as she could stand.

After her shower, some of the soreness had left, but she didn't know how she was going to be able to get on her horse later.

Wearing her robe, she sat on the bed and looked at the room service menu. She picked up the phone and dialed. "I'd like to order breakfast. Could you bring me a Garden Omelet, whole-wheat toast, and coffee? Thank you." After confirming the order and room number she hung up and moved to the desk to check her email and read the news on her laptop.

A short time later and after dressing, there was a knock at the door. A young lady brought in Grace's breakfast.

"Thank you," she said. After signing the bill, the girl left.

Before sitting down to eat, Grace looked through her purse for some Aspirin, but found none. "Maybe the coffee will help," she said aloud.

After breakfast, she headed over to the ranch for her trail ride. Inside the main office, she looked around to see if they had anything for her soreness.

"Can I help you?" The young lady from the other day was back behind the counter.

"Hi, I have a riding lesson at ten with Andy, but I really need some Aspirin or Ibuprofen right now."

"There's a rack on that counter in the corner. Most people need something after their first day of riding." She pointed toward the front of the office next to the window.

Grace pulled out a foil packet with two pills, got a bottle of water out of the cooler, and paid the lady. "I thought I was in good shape, but I think I was wrong."

"Horseback riding will do that to you."

Grace tore open the packet and swallowed the pills with a drink of water.

"Andy should be out front soon," the young blonde said. "He's a pretty good teacher, isn't he?"

"I suppose. I don't really need much in the way of lessons. I used to ride a lot, but am kind of rusty."

"He's the best we have here at the ranch, in more ways than just riding, if you know what I mean." She blushed.

Grace wondered if she were bragging, or just stupid to be talking like that to a customer. "I'll wait for him on the porch."

She didn't even have time to sit down before Andy stepped onto the porch. "Morning. How are you today?" he asked.

"I'm fine and ready for the ride. Oh, here's your jacket from last night. I forgot to give it back to you before you left."

"Thanks." He stuffed it into his saddlebag.

She couldn't help but stare at the derriere his jeans hugged so tightly. "We're going on a mountain trail today, right?"

"Sort of. I'm going to take you on the northwest trail that goes up into the hills, but not all the way into the mountains. I thought we'd tackle the harder trail tomorrow."

"Okay. Let's get started."

Andy had tied the horses up to the post in front of the office. She saw Rosebud, the same horse she had yesterday, but he had a different horse today. "You're not riding Ricochet?"

"No, she's getting on in years and the northwest trail might be a little too much for her. This is Whiskey."

Grace giggled. "How appropriate. I recall you kind of liked to drink whiskey back in school."

"I was stupid back then and did a lot of things I shouldn't have."

"We both did." She changed the subject before he could respond. "I hope I can get on her. I'm a little sore."

"I'll help you."

Before she could protest, he had his hands on her waist and gave her a lift up, and she mounted the horse. "Thanks."

He got on his horse and they headed off in the opposite direction as yesterday. "Do you know what trail you'll be taking next weekend on the ride with your co-workers?"

"No, but I'm sure it will be an easy one since some of them have never ridden before."

"So, if it will be an easy ride and you've ridden before, I don't understand why you needed to brush up on your skills. From what I could see, you're riding just like your old self."

"I told you. They know I've won riding awards and I didn't want to look like a fool to them."

"Since when have you cared how you look to someone else?"

"I'm not the wild teenage girl that you used to know."

"No ma'am, you are not. You have turned into a beautiful, strong, confident, sexy woman."

She pulled up on the reins to stop her horse. "Let's get one thing straight right now. I let you hold me while we danced last night and I let you walk me back to my hotel, but nothing else. You don't have the right to call me sexy anymore." He would have to earn the right to call her that again.

"Sorry. I didn't mean anything by it except as a compliment," he replied.

"Well, I just want to get that out in the open right now."

"Noted." He gave his horse a little kick and they started up the trail again.

"Is that blonde in the ranch office your girlfriend?" She regretted asking it almost immediately.

This time Andy pulled up his horse and stopped. "And, you think you have the right to ask me that?"

"No. You're right, I don't." She started off ahead of him on the trail.

He kicked his horse and caught up to her. "No, she's not my girlfriend. Why do you ask?"

"She made sure I knew you were not available, as if I wanted you."

"She's the boss' daughter and all the guys have, well, shall I say, dated her."

"Does she know you're a love'em and leave'em kind of guy?"

"What? Wait just a minute. I'm not the one that ran off to Colorado Springs after graduation and never called or wrote. I believe the love'em and leave'em tag should go on you."

"There was no reason to keep in touch. We weren't coming back to Summit, so why keep in contact?"

"I guess I don't understand how you could just forget us and all the great times we spent together."

"I had my reasons."

"What reasons?"

"You wouldn't understand." They reached an area of the trail that opened up to a view of the mountains to the west. The spring thaw had yet to occur in the high country and the tops of the peaks were still snow-covered. She took out her cell phone and took a picture. "There's no place on earth more beautiful than Colorado."

"I know. That's one reason I don't regret ever leaving here," he said.

"You wanted to go to college and study computer programming so you could get out of here. What happened?"

"A change of heart, I guess. Come on, we have a ways to go before we reach the halfway mark." He turned his horse away from the view, and headed up the trail with Grace following.

Forty-five minutes later, they reached the midway point of the ride. "We need to get off here and let the horses have a break before we start back down," Andy said.

Grace got down off of Rosebud.

"Have you worked out the soreness yet?"

"Yes, I think I have, but the pain pills I took before we left probably has something to do with that."

"You're probably right." Like yesterday, he opened his saddlebag and got out a snack and two bottles of water for them, and an apple for each horse. "Here you go."

"A sandwich today?"

"It's a longer ride and Bobby knew I was taking you today. He said he made something special."

She opened the bag with the sandwich inside and found a ham and cheese with tomato, lettuce, and dressing. Andy did the same. "That was nice of Bobby."

"He makes that dressing himself. It's his secret recipe and really good too."

Grace took a bite. "Oh my gosh, it's delicious and I never thought I would say that about a ham sandwich."

Andy laughed and gave the apples to the horses before he sat down to eat. "Do you ever think about moving back here?" he asked.

"I doubt it. My job's in Denver and I've worked so hard to get to where I am. I can't imagine leaving to move back to the country. Do you ever think about leaving?"

"Nope. I want to raise a family here. I can't think of a better place to do that."

Grace suddenly had a shiver.

"Are you cold?"

"No, I don't know why I did that," she lied.

"My dad gave me twenty acres of his ranch and someday I'll build a big house there to raise a family."

"That sounds nice."

"You're a marketing person, right?" he asked.

"I'm a Marketing Consultant, but I hope to eventually work my way to Director of the Marketing Department."

"I heard the new ski resort that's opening up is looking for a Marketing Director."

"Really? That's interesting." Grace nibbled on her sandwich while pondering the possibility of running her own department in her home town, and being so close to Andy again.

"I know you just got divorced, but don't you want to have a family?" Andy interrupted her thoughts.

Grace had just taken a drink, and nearly spewed water all over Andy. "Don't you think we should be heading back? I bet you have another ride to guide this afternoon." She did not want to talk about having a family, especially with Andy.

He looked at his watch. "I suppose we should." He picked up the sandwich bags and water bottles to stow in his saddlebag. "Do you need help getting on your horse again?"

"No, I think I can do it." She placed her foot in the stirrup, grasped the saddle horn, and pulled herself upon the saddle.

Andy did the same and they started down the trail riding side by side. "Tomorrow, we'll head up into the mountains for a longer ride since it will be your last. I'm booked in the morning, would an afternoon ride around two-o'clock be okay?"

"That actually works really well because I'm having lunch at noon with Cindy."

"When are you heading back to Denver?"

"I'll be driving back after our ride tomorrow and then I'll be back on Friday for my company's retreat."

"Would you like to have dinner with me tonight?" he asked.

She hadn't expected that. "I...probably should spend the evening getting packed. Maybe another time."

"Come on, Gracie. It'll just be dinner between two old friends."

"It's not a good idea and I've asked you to not call me Gracie anymore."

"What do you mean, not a good idea?"

"It's just not. Can we leave it at that?"

"I suppose we'll have to." He gave his horse a nudge and went ahead of Grace on the trail.

She knew she'd probably made him angry, but spending the evening with Andy, even for just a dinner, would bring back too many memories. Memories that she would like to forget. If she could get through one more day with him, she wouldn't have to see him again, and wouldn't have to worry about him finding out her secret.

Very little conversation occurred for the rest of the ride. If he said anything, it had to do with riding the horse or maneuvering the trail.

Once back at the stable, Andy dismounted. Grace had no problem getting down off this time, and turned to find herself trapped between him and her horse. She could feel Andy's warm breath on her face.

"I don't understand what I've done or haven't done to make you act the way you have, but whatever it was, I'm sorry."

A stable boy came over and took the reins from Grace, then led Rosebud to a stall where he unsaddled her.

Grace could now take a step back away from him. "It's not anything you did or didn't do. I just have a lot on my mind." She turned to leave.

"Two o'clock tomorrow, don't forget."

She waved back at him without turning around. Once in her car and on the road back to the hotel, her face felt flushed, and she fought to hold back her tears. "One more day, I just need to get through one more day."

Grace spent the rest of the afternoon doing work in her hotel room. She had planned on ordering room service for dinner that evening, but when the time came, she couldn't bear to stay in the room one minute longer. She needed to get outside and away from her phone and computer. She decided to take a walk and see if she could find a small café near the hotel.

After changing clothes and putting on a little makeup, she headed out. Once out in front of the hotel, she turned left and walked up the street. It was a cool, but nice evening for a walk. The streets were partially full of people, probably also looking for a place to eat, or a club nearby for dancing.

She soon came upon a small intimate looking restaurant that didn't look too busy. She entered and asked the hostess for a quiet table where she could eat alone, and was seated in a corner booth at the rear of the main room. She ordered iced tea and a salad and did some people-watching as she waited for her food.

One table had an older couple, probably around her parents' age. She could tell by their facial expressions that they were in a deep discussion about something.

Seated at another table was a younger couple obviously in love. They sat next to each other with their hands constantly touching; star-crossed lovers never taking their eyes off of each other.

Grace remembered being that way once, not with her ex-husband, but with Andy. They were so young back then, teenagers actually, and they did foolish things like all teenagers do. Regrets.

She only had one.

The waitress approached and placed Grace's salad in front of her and started to leave. "Could I go ahead and have my bill, please?"

"It's been taken care of," the waitress replied.

"What do you mean?"

"That gentleman at the bar paid your bill." She was pointing to Andy, who sat on a stool at the end of the bar, and raised his beer bottle toward her. He got up and walked over.

"Mind if I sit down?" he asked.

"I suppose I should thank you for paying for my dinner?"

"You don't have to." He still stood.

"You might as well sit down."

He slid on the other side of the booth from her.

"Aren't you going to order something to eat?"

"Bobby fixed a meal for us at the ranch and I already ate. Is that all you're going to have?"

"It's all I need."

"I couldn't function on rabbit food."

"Of course you couldn't. You need more protein to keep your energy up for your rides. I bet Bobby has plenty of meat and vegetables for your meals, doesn't he?"

"Yeah, every meal is like that. Grace, what are we doing talking about food? Something is going on between us and I don't know what it is."

"I don't know what you're talking about. You're imagining

things."

"I don't think so, but I can tell you still don't want to talk about it." He got up from the booth. "I'll see you tomorrow."

She wanted to stop him. She wanted to tell him, but she knew he wouldn't understand or forgive her, so she let him go.

After that, she didn't feel much like finishing her meal. She put some money down for her tip and went outside for the walk back to the hotel. The streets were even less crowded now and just as she walked past the entrance to an ally, a man stepped out in front of her.

"Hello there, darling."

He startled her. "Hello." She could smell stale beer on him and she started to step to the right to get around him, but he moved in front of her again.

"Where ya going?" he asked.

"Back to my hotel." She moved to the left and he mirrored her. He could easily drag her into the ally and no one would know. That's when she heard footsteps coming up from behind her.

"Is there a problem?" It was Andy, who now stood next to her.

"I was just offering to walk the lady back to her hotel. A pretty thing like her shouldn't be out on the street alone," the man said.

"She's not alone, so you can go crawl back into your hole."

For just a few seconds, it became a staring contest between the two men with the stranger finally taking a step back, turning, and crossing the street.

She turned to Andy. "Thank you. I don't know what would have happened if you hadn't been there." She thought for a second. "Wait a minute. Were you waiting for me?"

"That guy was right. It's not safe for you to walk out here alone. I was waiting for you so I could make sure you made it back to your hotel safely and it's a good thing I did."

She didn't say anything.

"Come on, I'll walk you the rest of the way," he said.

"Okay. I guess that's probably a good idea."

They walked the rest of the way to the hotel, with her stopping in front of the lobby door. "I can make it the rest of the way myself."

"Not this time. I'm walking you all the way to your room."

She didn't protest. She knew it wouldn't do any good. He was always a man who honored the women he was with. She had always felt safe when she was with him. Maybe too safe, she recalled.

They stepped off of the elevator and walked down to her room. At her door, she turned to him and found him standing way too close to her. The scent of his cologne nearly put her into a trance. "Thank you again," she said.

"I'm glad I could help. I don't think you'll have any problems now that you're back to your room."

She took her key card out of her purse. She had an urge to kiss him and she was sure he had the same thought. Before either of them could do that, she put her card in the door slot and opened the door. "I'll see you tomorrow." She stepped into her room and closed the door.

Chapter Three

Grace got up early the next morning and packed so she could checkout of the hotel before meeting Cindy for lunch. Upon doing that, she asked the front desk if she could leave her luggage there while she had lunch, and they obliged.

When she stepped into the hotel's restaurant she spotted Cindy at a table and joined her.

"I'm glad we could have lunch before you left town," Cindy said as Grace sat down.

"Me too. I hope you don't mind, but I ordered the special for both of us. I'm a little pressed for time today, sorry."

"That's fine. I don't mind at all."

"Have you enjoyed your visit home?"

"It was nice seeing you and your dad. I only wish I hadn't run into Andy."

"I know you two ended your relationship when you left town, but that was a long time ago. What happened that was so bad you still don't want to see him? Honestly, I don't think Andy even knows the reason you broke up."

The waitress brought their food and drinks and set it down in front of them.

"I know it was a long time ago, but I really don't want to talk about it. This looks really good." She avoided answering and changed the subject. Luckily, Cindy didn't press for more information as they continued their lunch.

"Will you be returning early on Friday for your corporate retreat?"

"My company is renting a bus to bring all of us up together. I think we leave Denver around one-o'clock. We have one meeting, sort of an orientation right after we arrive and get checked in, then we don't have anything until the next day."

"If you need anything at all while you're here, just let me know. I want to make sure you get VIP treatment."

"Thanks. Andy told me that some company is building a ski resort this summer. What does the town think about that?"

"Mostly everyone thinks it's great. It will mean more jobs for people and more business for the stores and hotels, but there's always a few that are against it. They don't want more people in town."

"With just the few new places that have sprung up since I left seems to have really made the town grow."

"It has, but a few of the older people in town don't like that. So many smaller businesses have closed, just like where the hardware store used to be. Of course, the owners eventually sold the building and made lots of money."

"And, the Buck Creek Ranch, as I remember that used to just be a horse ranch. Now, they've built a hotel, restaurant, and stables. That's incredible."

"They employ a lot of locals and even more people during the summer. It kept Andy from leaving town."

"What?"

"You remember, he was thinking about going to college to study computer technology."

"I remember."

"A couple months after we graduated, a big company came in and bought the ranch and started converting it into what it is now. They needed people to work with the horses and Andy gave up on college to do that."

"He didn't tell me that. He told me yesterday that he wanted to stay here and raise a family."

"That's probably right. He's really worked his way up at the ranch. He may be your trail guide, but he supervises all the guides and they don't do anything to the horses there unless Andy approves it. If he had gotten his degree, he probably would have ended up like you and worked for a company in Denver. The same thing would have happened to me. I would probably be working in hospitality at a ski resort myself instead of coming back home."

"So, the companies coming into Summit likely have saved the town."

"I think so. Oh goodness, look at the time, I need to get going. I have a meeting to get to." Both ladies stood and hugged. "I'm so glad you came into town early so we could get together."

"I am too. Here's my card and I wrote my home address and personal email on the back. We should really keep in touch," Grace said.

"We will. I've already taken care of the bill. See you on Friday."

"Thanks." Grace sat back down at the table after Cindy left.

She thought about her old life in Summit and how things had changed so much since then. She often wondered how her life would be, if things hadn't gone the way they did. Would she still be living in Summit? Would she and Andy be married? She shook that thought right out of her head. She just wanted to get the day over with and leave town. With any luck, when she came back on the weekend, she wouldn't even see Andy.

After taking one more sip of her drink, Grace left the restaurant, retrieved her luggage from the front desk, and headed to her car to drive to the stables for her last ride.

The stables were busier than usual when she arrived. She parked her car at the end of the parking area in front of the ranch office and immediately spotted Andy standing in front of the building when she got out of the car. He met her halfway.

"Afternoon. Are you ready for your last ride?" he asked.

"I am."

"I'm glad you came a little early. The weather may get rainy late this afternoon and I don't want to get stuck up on the mountain, if it does. The horses are already saddled in the barn and ready to go."

"Let's get this over with." Grace started toward the barn.

"Gee, I love your enthusiasm," he called after her.

She ignored him.

Andy followed her to the barn and made sure she had no trouble getting up on her horse. He then mounted his horse, and she followed him out of the back door of the barn.

"We're going on a trail that should be familiar to you," he said

"Which trail is that?"

"We're going on the Half-face Camp Trail."

She pulled her horse up. "Why that trail?"

"You always loved riding that trail for the view of the valley."

She nudged her horse and started forward again. That was also the trail that as teens, she and Andy used to ride when they wanted to make love and not get caught.

46

They had ridden in silence for about thirty minutes and had finally reached the beginning of the trail. "Do you want to take the lead?" he asked.

"No, you're the trail guide. You should go first."

"The trail is wide enough to ride side by side."

"I know." Grace moved her horse up next to him.

"Tell me about your job?" he asked.

"I told you yesterday that I'm a Marketing Consultant for the Myers Corporation."

"That doesn't tell me anything. What do you do all day?"

"My staff and I are responsible for a lot of the advertising for the company. We manage the web site, magazine ads, press releases, and also write up training materials. Most people think it's boring stuff, but I love doing it."

"That doesn't sound boring. It sounds like a lot of responsibility. I'm surprised they let you leave this week."

"They only agreed to it as long as I participated in a couple meetings via a phone call. I've actually been doing a lot of work in my hotel room while I've been here."

"Don't you get vacation time?"

"I do, but usually don't use it. I can't be away for very long."

The trail narrowed and Grace slowed her horse to follow behind Andy. "Oh come on. I'm sure you're good at what you do, but there's surely people there that can pick up the slack, if you take some time off."

"There is, but I want to make sure everything is done right and I can't guarantee that if I'm not there."

"You always did have to be in control."

"What do you mean by that?"

"When we were dating in high school, we always had to do what you wanted. You never wanted to do anything I suggested."

"That's not true."

He stopped his horse and turned in his saddle to look at her. "Oh yeah, name one thing that we did together that was my idea."

"Well, there was." She paused. "What about the time..." She stopped again to think. "Oh, I don't know. That was a long time ago." She gave her horse a little kick and trotted around Andy and headed on up the trail.

"See, you still have to be in control," he called after her.

An hour later, they reached the summit of the ride and got off of the horses to rest. Andy got the sandwiches and water bottles out of his saddlebag and handed Grace her lunch. They both sat on the bench that overlooked the valley below.

"Thanks." She opened her bottle of water and took a big drink. "Do you really think I have to be in control?"

Andy swallowed. "I only know that back in high school, you had to make all the decisions for the group."

"No one ever disagreed."

"No one wanted to argue with you. They knew they wouldn't win. Hell, you were even in control whenever we had sex." He chuckled.

In the distance, a faint rumble of thunder could be heard coming from behind the mountain. Grace sat on the bench and finished her sandwich while Andy got some carrots out to give to the horses.

"I didn't realize I was like that back then."

"What about now? You know it now right?"

"I supposed it's partly why my marriage failed. I didn't want to give in to his ideas about us."

"So, you've changed since learning that."

Suddenly, a line of clouds came over the mountain hiding the sun.

"I'm trying. I've-" she paused. "I went through some things after my family and I moved from here that sort of reinforced my control issues."

He gave the last carrot to the horses and walked over to sit next to her. "Are you talking about losing your horse?"

"Partly." She got up and took a few steps away.

He got up and walked behind her, placing his hand on her shoulder. "Gracie, if you need to talk about anything, I'd be glad to listen."

She stepped away from his touch, took a deep breath, and turned. "I'm fine."

He went back to the bench and sat down. "Did Cindy tell you that we have a class reunion coming up soon?"

"No, she didn't mention it." She bent over and picked a couple wild flowers and took a sniff of their scent.

"You should try to come back for it. I know everyone would love to see you."

A cold breeze kicked up and another crack of thunder, much closer this time, boomed around them.

Andy looked at the sky. "This doesn't look good. I think that weather front is coming faster than they thought. We need to head back." He quickly gathered their trash and stowed it back in the saddlebag. Grace threw down her flowers and ran to her horse and got on. Andy had already mounted his when a streak of lightening hit on the ridge above them, and instantaneously a clap of thunder shook the ground.

"Come on!" he took off with Grace following.

The rain fell hard making the trail too slippery for the horses to gallop fast. With the heavy cloud cover, darkness came early. Andy pulled his horse up and Grace stopped next to him.

"We have to find shelter somewhere!" he yelled over the sound of the rain beating down.

Grace held her hand above her eyes to try and shield the stinging rain from her face. "Isn't there an old cabin somewhere on the other side of those trees?" she shouted back.

Andy nodded. "I think there is, and a barn too. Let's try and find it." He pulled the horse's reins to the right and they headed through the trees.

The cold rain had already soaked through Grace's light jacket and clothes, and she could feel the shift in temperature. Finally, they came out of the trees in a very small cove with an old cabin and barn next to it.

"There it is," Andy called. Both of them kicked their horses and quickly raced to the cabin. They jumped off the horses and Andy went to see if they could get into the cabin. The door opened. Grace stood on the porch next to him. "Go ahead in and I'll put the horses in the barn. I'll be in as soon as I make sure they're secure for the night."

Grace did what Andy said while he led the horses to the barn. She found the inside of the cabin completely bare except for a couch and some wood stacked inside. She wanted to take her wet jacket off, but she was freezing. She went into what she figured was the kitchen in search of matches to start a fire. She found none. A sound in the room told her Andy had come in, and she went back to the front room.

"Did you find anything?" he asked.

"I looked through the drawers in there for some matches, but didn't find anything."

He sat down his saddlebags next to the fireplace. "I have a lighter."

"I'm so glad. There's some wood over there."

He got his lighter out of the bag and looked through the wood. "These pieces are too big to light on their own. Did you see anything we can use for kindling?"

"No."

"I'm going back out to the barn and see if I can find anything we can use."

He went out the door back into the rain, and Grace sat down on the hearth of the fireplace and started shivering. Grace feared storms since being a child, but for some reason, she wasn't afraid during this one since she knew Andy would keep her safe.

Andy came back in carrying an ax. "Look what I found." He immediately started splitting a piece of wood into smaller pieces. "Here, put this in the fireplace." He gave her a handful of straw from his pocket. "Place the kindling pieces on top like a little tent."

She did as instructed and stepped back. Once Andy finished splitting the wood, he put the rest of it on what she had built. He pulled out his lighter and kneeled in front of the tinder to light the straw. When it lit, he started blowing on the flame to help the fire burn better.

Grace was relieved, but still cold when she finally saw a glow in the fireplace and the smoke drawing up into the chimney.

Andy picked up a couple of the smaller pieces of wood and gently placed them on the fire. It didn't take long for the sound of the crackling fire to fill the room.

"Come on over here and warm up," Andy said.

Grace shuffled over and sat on the stone hearth with her arms wrapped around her.

Andy got a portable radio out of his saddlebag. "Buck Creek, this is Andy. Is anyone around?"

"Go ahead, Andy. Where are you?" Grace recognized Mr. Watkins' voice coming over the radio.

"We got caught in the storm up on Half-face Camp Trail and took shelter at the old Barrett farm. We're okay, and will wait it out here until morning."

"Sounds like a plan. The storm should be past by then. Stay warm, the temps are going to drop and the rain is going to change to snow later tonight."

"Thanks, Hank. We've got a fire going already. See you in the morning."

Andy turned off the radio and placed it on the floor next to his saddlebag. "You're shivering."

She was so cold her teeth rattled. "You're cold too," she noticed.

"We need to get out of these wet clothes."

"Not a chance. I'll stay here by the fire. It won't take long to get dry and warm up."

"You can't do that, Gracie. It will take too long and hypothermia will set in."

"Stop calling me that! I'm not your Gracie anymore." She wanted to get up and walk away from him, but she was too cold to leave the fire.

Andy got up and left the room. When he returned, he carried two blankets and handed one to Grace. "Take those wet clothes off and wrap up in this. We need to dry our clothes by the fire."

"I'm not taking my clothes off."

"If you don't, you're going to get sick. Now, go into the other room and take all of your clothes off and wrap up in this." He tossed the blanket into her lap. "I'm going to strip off right here so unless you want to gaze upon my naked body, I suggest you go into the other room to undress." He started to unzip his pants.

"I'm going." She stomped into the other room. She started removing her wet clothes. He had some nerve bossing her around like that. On the other hand, his quick thinking had probably saved both of them from a very uncomfortable and dangerous ride back down the mountain.

She finished undressing and went back into the main room placing her clothes on the rock hearth. Andy added a couple more pieces of wood onto the fire. His clothes were lying on the hearth and he had wrapped himself in the other blanket.

"Come sit down. You can't stand up all night."

She walked over and sat down on the couch as far from him as she could.

"Are you hungry? I have some snacks stuff in my saddlebag."

"Not really."

He got up and pulled some granola bars out of his saddlebag and sat back down. "You really should eat something. It will help warm you."

She reached over and took one of the bars from him.

He tore open the wrapper on his and began eating. "Sorry, we don't have any bottles of water left."

"That's okay. How long will it take for the clothes to dry?"

"I'm not sure. They were pretty wet. Once those rocks get warm, it should help. I'm sure they'll be dry by morning."

In the glow of the fire, she knew he could read the concern on her face. There was no way he understood why she kept acting the way she did around him.

The sun had long set and the wind whistled as it blew around the outside of the cabin. Suddenly, there was a loud bang outside.

Grace jumped. "What was that?"

Andy got up and looked out the window. "Damn, the barn door blew open. I have to go close and latch it."

"Wearing that?"

"I'll have to put my wet clothes back on." He started dressing.

"It's too cold out there, you'll freeze."

"I'm not going out there naked. I can't let the horses get too cold. I'll be fine. I may be a while if the latch broke on the barn door, Keep the fire going."

He rushed out and closed it behind him.

Andy had been gone for around thirty minutes when he burst back in through the door.

"Oh my gosh, you look like an icicle." She put her arm around him and guided him over to the fire.

"It's. Snowing. Outside." He tried to talk, but was shivering too bad.

"Your lips are blue," she said.

"You. Should. See. My. Other. Parts," he joked and she laughed.

"You need to get out of those wet clothes."

She rubbed his shoulders through the blanket to help try to warm him.

"I've got to sit down. I feel like I'm going to pass out."

She guided him to the couch where they both sat. This time, she positioned herself next to him. He still shivered, but not quite as bad.

Suddenly, his body went limp.

* * * *

When he woke up, he was still on the couch and Grace was asleep against him. Skin to skin, they were both under the blankets together.

He saw her looking up at him. "How long was I out?" he asked.

"About an hour, I guess."

"How did we end up like this?"

"You were turning blue and I couldn't get you closer to the fire, so I had to use my body to warm you. I had to take your wet clothes off of you. I was so scared. I thought I was going to lose you."

Andy put his arm around her and looked into her eyes. "You probably did save my life."

She didn't say anything, just moved closer and kissed him. Her lips were so warm against his own that it sent a pulse throughout his body.

He began kissing her back, suckling them. She parted her lips allowing his tongue to enter and claim her mouth.

It surprised him that she didn't pull away. Instead, he felt her hand begin to caress his chest. He became very aware that his member was becoming hard, especially when she started moving her hand downward. He grasped it before it reached its destination.

"Do you know what you're doing?" he whispered.

"I do. I need this, Andy."

"You're sure?"

She nodded her head.

He captured her lips again and with his hand found her hardening nipple. She jumped when he touched it.

He then took the same route she had started with him and moved his hand down her body. She let out a moan when he tickled the inside of her thigh, and arched her back when he found her sweet mound. She dug her fingers into his back, pulling him closer and wrapping her legs around him.

He entered one finger into her moist depth and it brought him to the edge. He removed his hand and plunged himself into her. "Oh, Gracie," he whispered in to her ear. Both shivered with excitement as their bodies fell into a rhythm. It didn't take long for both of them to climax together with him taking one last thrust into her.

He collapsed on top of her and they both panted to catch their breath. Without either saying a word, Andy moved to next to her and pulled the blanket up over them, and both fell asleep.

The next morning, Andy woke up alone on the couch. He rolled over and saw that Grace's clothes were gone from the hearth. He sat up on the couch and saw her looking out of the window.

"I thought you were gone." He stood, and wrapping the blanket around his waist, walked over to her and touched her shoulder. She flinched.

"Grace? What's wrong?"

"It was a mistake, another mistake." She turned and tears rolled down her cheeks.

He tried to take her into his arms, but she walked away.

"What is going on?"

"We shouldn't have done that last night." She started to walk away from him.

With one hand holding the blanket on, he grabbed her arm with the other. "You said you wanted to. I don't get it. Were you just teasing me?"

"No. Please let go."

He released her.

"Tell me what then."

"Put your clothes on and I'll explain."

Andy picked up his dry clothes and got dressed. "Okay, so tell me."

Grace sat on the couch. "I should have told you a long time ago."

He moved over and sat on the hearth in front of her. "Just tell me."

"When my family and I moved away from here after high school, I was pregnant."

"What?"

She continued. "My parents didn't know it at the time. If they did, my dad would have never taken that job and we would have stayed. I couldn't ruin his career, so I waited until after we got settled and told them."

"Grace, you were pregnant with my child?"

"Yes." She lowered her head.

Andy stood and took a few steps before he turned back to her. "Where's the child now?"

She began sobbing. "When I was thrown from that horse, I lost the baby," she cried. "I'm sorry, Andy."

"You're sorry? You—" He stopped himself and walked over to the window.

Grace composed herself. "I know now that I should have told you back then."

"Why didn't you tell me after you told your parents? You must have known that I would have married you. I loved you, Grace."

"Mom and Dad wanted me to tell you, but I couldn't ruin your life like that."

"Ruin my life? You've got to be kidding. Didn't you think I would eventually find out I had a child? Or, didn't you want the child? Is that why you were out riding while you were pregnant? You hoped something would happen?"

"No. I was going to have it."

Andy snatched up his jacket and saddlebags. "I'll go saddle the horses and we can be on our way back down the mountain." He slammed the door behind him when he went out.

A short time later, he brought the horses to the front of the cabin and tied them to the railing. He came back inside and not saying a word, checked to make sure the fire was out and all of their trash picked up. He went to the door and stood with it open, waiting for Grace to walk outside. She did so and they both mounted their horses. Andy led the way with Grace following him, and neither uttered a word on the ride back to the ranch.

Once in the barn, Grace jumped off the horse and headed straight to her car. "Grace, wait," he called after her.

She paid no attention to him, got in her car, and left.

Chapter Four

The next evening, Andy walked into the Silver Bullet Saloon with one thing on his mind, and when he saw her, he headed straight to her table.

"Cindy, I need to talk to you." He didn't so much as crack a smile.

Chuck stood. "What's going on, Andy?"

Andy took a deep breath to relax some and looked at Cindy. "Can I sit down? I really need to talk to you."

"Sure. Please, sit. What's going on?" Cindy said.

Both Andy and Chuck sat down.

"Grace told me something, something that happened in high school and I want to know if you knew about it."

"What is it?"

At that moment, Bobby walked up to the table and sat a beer on the table in front of Andy. "I figured you'd order this."

"Thanks, Bobby. I definitely need it."

"Did you all hear about Andy's exciting night last night?" Bobby asked.

"No, what happened?" Chuck asked.

"He and that pretty Grace were stranded on the mountain in last night's storm. I can only imagine what went on in that cabin."

"Thanks for the beer,   Bobby. Put it on my tab," Andy said.

Bobby must have understood Andy's meaning because he walked away.

"Andy?" Cindy inquired.

He took off his cowboy hat and placed it on the empty chair at the table. "Grace and I had a late afternoon trail ride and got caught in the storm that hit. We stayed the night in the old Barrett cabin. We were wet. We were cold."

He saw the look on Cindy's face, that look of disappointment.

"I didn't take advantage of her. It was mutual. The next morning, Grace acted different, distant. I kept prodding to find out what was wrong and she finally told me."

"What was it?"

"Cindy, did you know, did Grace ever tell you, that she was pregnant when her and her family moved away from here?"

"What? Pregnant? I had no idea. After she moved away, she never answered any of my letters or emails."

"She told me that her parents didn't even know until they had settled in Colorado Springs. She begged her parents not to notify me because she didn't want to hold me back with a baby."

Chuck put his hand on Andy's shoulder. "That had to be tough to hear."

"Where's the child now?" Cindy asked.

Andy wiped his eyes with his shirtsleeve and sort of chuckled in a weird way. "She lost it when she was thrown from a horse. Karma, eh?"

"Oh Andy, I'm so sorry."

He looked at Cindy. "You remember how lost I was after she left. I loved her and wanted to spend the rest of my life with her. We could have had children together, been a family." He took a drink of his beer.

"It sounds like she was only thinking of you and your future by not telling you. She knew at the time what you wanted and it wasn't staying here."

"She still should have told me!"

"Yes, she should have. I just mean that it sounds like she had your best interest at heart."

"Have you tried to call and talk to her since she went back to Denver?" Chuck asked.

"I tried several times, it always goes to voicemail and she hasn't returned my calls."

"Have you thought about how she probably feels?" Cindy asked. "I'm sure she feels responsible for losing the baby. She was so in love with you back then. That baby would have been a part of you that she would have had forever. I'm sure she was devastated."

"If that were true, why was she riding? Why would she have taken chances like that?"

"You know as well as I do that there's nothing wrong with a pregnant woman riding a horse, especially early on in the pregnancy. You've even told me about having pregnant women on some of your trail rides."

He sat silent for a few minutes. "Do you know when she's coming back with her company employees?"

"They're due to check in around noon tomorrow. I think they're chartering a bus for the drive up."

"Thanks." He took one last drink of his beer and stood up.

"Are you going to talk to her?" Cindy asked.

"I don't intend to ever speak to her again." He picked up his hat, threw down some money, and walked out of the bar.

* * * *

By the time Cindy reached the front door of the hotel, the occupants of the bus had received their luggage and were entering the lobby. She directed them to the front desk clerk handling their room assignments, and at the same time was watching for Grace. She finally saw her standing next to three other beautiful women, and made her way out to them.

"Grace, I'm so glad you made it."

"Hi, Cindy." She gave her a hug. "I'd like for you to meet my friends. This is Silvia, Maria, and Lucy. Ladies, this is Cindy, my best friend from high school."

"Oh, I bet you could tell us some juicy stories about how Grace was in high school," the redheaded Lucy said.

"I bet I could too. In fact, I still hear stories about her even today." Cindy looked at Grace and knew by the look on her face that she knew exactly what she was talking about.

"Cindy is in charge of our whole retreat this weekend. Why don't you gals go check in and let me talk to Cindy about a few things. I'll meet you in the lobby."

The three ladies went inside and Grace pulled Cindy to the sidewalk. "Andy told you, didn't he?"

"He found Chuck and I at the bar last night. My gosh, he was devastated."

"You don't think I didn't feel that way too?"

"I'm sorry, Grace. Of course, you did, but you kept this from him, from all of your friends."

"I had my reasons."

"Andy told us."

"Look, it's over and done with. I've moved on and so should he."

"Grace, if you ever need to talk about it, don't hesitate to call me. You can trust that I won't tell anyone anything you say."

Grace let out a sigh. "I appreciate that, Cindy. Thank you." She started inside the hotel.

"But, you need to talk to Andy and square things with him," Cindy called after her.

After dinner that evening, Grace and her friends walked to the Purple Valley Tavern to have a few drinks. As with all bars, the room was crowded and the live band was loud. They found a table and were served drinks.

"Come on, Grace. We want to know more about growing up in a small town," Silvia said.

"It was okay, as long as you didn't mind everyone in town knowing your business," she replied.

"What did you do for fun?" Mari asked. "I swear; I would be so bored until I was old enough to go to a bar."

"It was boring and there was only a few bars in town then. If we wanted beer, we had to find someone who would buy it for us."

"Beer? You drank beer? I can't stand the taste. If I couldn't have a good white wine, I'd sooner go sober," Lucy added, picking up her wine glass and motioning for the waitress to bring another.

"Tell us about your boyfriend?" Maria teased. "You did have a high school sweetheart, didn't you?"

"Well, yes."

"What did he look like?" Silvia inquired.

"He was just an average guy."

Lucy's drink was served and she took a gulp. "Next question, how old were you when you lost your virginity?"

As Grace opened her mouth, someone behind her spoke. "She was sixteen."

She recognized that voice and turned to find Andy standing behind her.

"What are you doing here?"

"Grace, aren't you going to introduce us?" Lucy said, standing.

"He's not worth an introduction." She turned back to the table.

"I'm Lucy Marlow and you are?" She extended her hand and took his.

"Andy Granger, Grace's high school sweetheart."

"And, apparently the man she lost her virginity to," Lucy said, still holding his hand. "Would you like to join us? We'd love to hear stories about our Grace."

"No, he wouldn't." Grace stared at Andy.

He apparently got the message. "No, I can't. I just wanted to stop by and say hello." He pulled away from Lucy's grasp and walked back to the bar where he joined his buddies.

"Pity," Lucy said, watching him walk away. "Grace, he's hot as hell. Was he that good-looking   as a teenager?"

"We parted on bad terms, so I'd just as soon not talk about him."

"We understand," Silvia said.

"Now wait a minute. So, you have no interest in him?" Lucy asked.

"None."

"Then, you wouldn't mind if I went over and talked to him?"

Grace knew that meant Lucy would do everything she could to get him into bed tonight. But, what could she do? She had no claim to him, and, as soon as this weekend was over, she didn't plan on ever seeing him again. "Not at all. Talk to him all you want."

That's all Lucy needed to hear. She jumped up and sauntered over to the bar where Andy sat with his buddies.

"I can't believe you let her do that," Maria said. "You know what she has in mind."

"I have no feelings for him."

"That's not how it looked when you heard his voice behind you just now."

Grace looked over at Andy. Lucy already had her paws on him, rubbing his thigh, and his buddies looked like they were ready to pounce on her if given the chance. As she was turning her attention back to the table, she glanced at the door. "Look, James is here."

"You know he's had a crush on you since you started working at the office. He's been trying to get the courage to ask you out every since your divorce was final," Silvia said.

"I know. I think I'll go buy him a drink." Grace stood from the table and walked over to James.

"Grace, it's nice to see you here."

"I saw you come in and thought you might like to join Silvia, Maria and I for a drink."

"Well, I'd hate to impose."

"Nonsense. It will give me a chance to get to know you better." She took him by the arm and walked him over to the table. "Look who I found, girls."

The ladies and James exchanged greetings and he sat down next to Grace, who scooted her chair closer. They all ordered drinks.

"James, did you know this is Grace's hometown?" Silvia asked.

"No, I thought you were from Colorado Springs."

"I am, but lived here until I graduated from high school."

"She's also an accomplished horsewoman. You should stick close to her on the trail ride tomorrow," Maria suggested.

"Oh, I'm not going on the trail ride. I have to set up for the meeting afterward."

Grace was relieved to hear that. This ruse was for tonight only. She didn't want to carry it any further than this. "That's too bad," she said. "If you'll excuse me, I need to go to the restroom." She stood and headed to the back hallway that had the big green neon restroom sign above it.

When she walked out, she found Andy leaning against the wall, waiting. She started to walk past him.

"Why are you here?" he asked.

"What?"

"I thought you'd be at the Silver Bullet. That's why I came here, to avoid you."

"I thought you'd be there and I didn't want to run into you. As you can see, that didn't work out too well."

"We need to talk," he said.

"I said all I had to say yesterday morning."

"That was a pretty big shock for me. You've had all these years to process it, but I haven't. I'd like to talk about it."

"You'll have to talk about it with someone else, but please not with Lucy. I don't want anyone from my office to know."

She turned to leave the hallway, but Andy grabbed her by the arm to stop her. Just as he did that, James entered the hallway.

"What's going on? Take you hand off of her."

"This is none of your business, it's between Grace and I."

"James, it's okay," she said.

"No, I don't think it is."

He grabbed Andy by the arm, causing Andy to let go of Grace, and in one smooth motion nailed James right on his nose. The blow put James on the floor.

The bouncer came running into the hall. "What's going on?"

"Sorry, Tom. It was a reflex action. I'll leave," Andy said.

"That's probably a good idea."

Andy looked back at Grace. Don't leave town until we talk." He walked away slinging his hand trying to shake off the pain.

Grace helped James up from the floor. "Are you okay?"

"I'm fine." He pulled his handkerchief from his pocket, wiped his nose, and found blood. "Maybe I need to go into the restroom for a few minutes."

"That's probably a good idea."

James went into the restroom and Grace walked back to her table to join her friends.

"Is James all right?" Silvia asked.

"He's got a bloody nose, but I think he'll be fine. Where's Lucy?" Grace started looking around the bar.

"After she saw your old boyfriend hit James, she rushed right over to him. She left with him and his friends," Maria explained.

"I think I've had just about all the excitement I can handle tonight. I'm going back to the hotel."

"We'll go with you," Silvia said.

"What about James?" Maria reminded them.

"He's a big boy. He found his way to the bar and he can find his way back to the hotel."

As the ladies walked back, Grace kept looking around for Andy, hoping that Lucy hadn't pulled him into a dark corner somewhere.

"What happened in that hallway, Grace?" Silvia asked.

"Oh, not much. Andy wanted to talk to me about something and I didn't feel like talking. James walked in just as Andy grabbed my arm to keep me from leaving. Things just went crazy."

"That Andy sure is nice looking. Did he look that good in high school?"

She took a deep breath. "Yeah, he did."

When they reached the hotel, Grace's friends weren't ready to go to their rooms yet. "Let's check out the bar here," Silvia suggested.

"That sounds like a great idea. It's still early. What do you think, Grace?

"Maybe just for a few minutes." She wanted to see if Lucy had dragged Andy to the hotel bar.

They walked in and found a table with several of their other co-workers and sat down. Grace looked around and didn't see Lucy or Andy anywhere.

When the topic of Andy and what had happened at the other bar came up, Grace decided it was time to go to her room. "If you all will excuse me, I'm really tired and would like to get some rest. I'll see you tomorrow."

Everyone said goodbye and Grace went to the elevator. She looked around the lobby while she waited, but didn't see Andy.

Up in her room, she sat on the bed and checked her cell phone for calls. She questioned why she was even thinking about him. Angry with herself, she took a shower and went to bed.

* * * *

The first thing on the schedule for the next morning was a company meeting. She entered the room and got herself a cup of coffee and a bagel. Looking around the room, she spotted her friends and headed toward their table. She saw Lucy talking a mile a minute as she approached, but by the time she reached the table Lucy had stopped.

"Good morning, Grace," Silvia said. All of the ladies

exchanged greetings as she sat down.

"How was your night after you left us, Lucy?" Grace asked.

"What? Last night? Well, I, ah, it was okay, I guess."

The look Maria gave to Grace let her know that there was more to Lucy's night than she was letting on. "Really? What did you do after you left us?"

"We did a little bar-hopping."

"I see."

"Look Grace, you said you didn't have any interest in him, so why shouldn't I have a little fun?"

"You can. Have all the fun with him that you want."

Just then, the man at the front of the room called the meeting to order and began his presentation. Just in the nick of time too.

Once they meeting had adjourned, everyone filed out of the room. Grace's friends waited for her in the hallway.

"Where are we supposed to go for the trail ride?" Maria asked.

"It says on our itinerary that we are supposed to meet in the lobby and someone will take us to the horses," Silvia said reading from a sheet of paper.

"This will be fun. The views that we'll see on the ride will be unbelievable," Grace explained.

They went to their rooms to change for the ride and met back in the lobby. They were there for only a few minutes when several cowboys and cowgirls came in and announced they were ready for the Myers Corporation group ride. The rest of the afternoon was spent on the trail.

After the ride, Grace and the other ladies walked back into the lobby of the hotel. On the way to the elevator, Grace heard someone call her name. She turned to see Cindy waving to her from down the hall. "I'll see you girls in the bar tonight?"

"Absolutely," Silvia replied.

The others got onto the elevator and Grace waited for Cindy to reach her.

"I'm so glad I caught you. Would you like to have dinner with me this evening?" Cindy asked.

"I'm supposed to meet the girls later for drinks at the bar, but I have no plans for dinner. I actually was going to just order room service, so yes dinner would be great."

"Wonderful, I figured this would be our last chance to get together before you go back to the city."

"You're probably right. I leave tomorrow and have no plans to come back here. It's not been a pleasant trip for me. What time do you want to meet?"

"How about seven? I'll have a table reserved in my name for us," Cindy said.

The elevator door open and a few people stepped out. "That sounds like a plan. I'll see you then." She stepped onto the elevator and went to her room.

That evening, Grace walked into the restaurant a little early and told the hostess she was dining with Cindy and a waitress seated her in one of the best tables in the room. After being served her cocktail, Cindy rushed in and sat down. "I'm sorry I'm late. It seems as though there's always an emergency when you want to get away." Cindy gave her drink order to the waitress and picked up the menu.

"It's the same at my office too."

"I wanted to make sure you knew that we're having a class reunion this summer and I'd love it if you could come. I know so many of the others would like to see you too."

"I don't know, it's hard to get away from work and well, Andy would probably be there and I really don't think I want to see him again."

"He's heartbroken, Grace. He's not been serious with any women since you and the thought that you two could have had a child together has really upset him. You should try and talk to him before you leave."

"Why? There's nothing we can say to each other to change things."

"He still cares so much about you."

"I've moved on. I live in Denver and he lives here. There's no future for us."

The waitress brought Cindy's cocktail and took their food order.

"I'm not saying that you have to take up where you left off, just open a dialogue with him."

"No, the memory's too painful. I thought I had put it past me, but coming here this week and seeing Andy again, it's brought all of that pain back. I just want to forget it again."

"But, it's not that easy, is it?" Cindy asked.

"No, it's not. I made the decision not to tell him about the baby to save him from being tied down. He had so many dreams and a baby would have ruined those dreams."

"You leaving ruined those dreams too."

"That wasn't my fault. My dad took that job away from here."

"I know. You can't change the past, but you can change the future. Just think about it, okay?" She reached across the table and gave Grace's hand a reassuring pat.

"I'll think about the reunion, but I won't make any promises."

"That's all I ask."

Grace and Cindy finished their meal talking about high school and what their classmates were doing now.

At nine o'clock, Cindy had to leave and Grace headed to the bar to meet her friends. At the doorway, she looked around the large room and finally spotted Maria waving to her from a back corner table. When she got to the table, she only saw Silvia and Maria.

"Where's Lucy?"

The two ladies looked at each other before answering. "She called me and said she had a date," Maria said.

Grace could tell something was up. "Who's her date with?"

Silvia blurted it out. "She said she had a date with your old boyfriend."

"Oh." She sat down and waved to the waiter. "Bring me a frozen margarita, please." Then, she looked at her friends who looked in shock. "Oh, you thought I'd be mad. Nonsense, Andy was my high school boyfriend. I'm long over him. Lucy can do whatever she wants with him." She may have fooled her friends, but inside she hated Lucy right now.

A few other co-workers, including James, joined them later in the evening. Grace had continued drinking margaritas and was finally reaching the point of feeling a little dizzy from it.

"I think I'm going to call it a night while I can still make it to my room on my own," she said.

"I'd be glad to make sure you make it there," James offered. The others made cat-calls at his comment, turning him a shade of red.

"Thanks, but I think I can make it okay."

She got up and left the bar, but in the lobby she felt the need for some fresh air before going up to her room, and stepped outside. She found a bench on the sidewalk in front of the hotel and sat down. The night was beautiful, a little cool with a clear sky.

She shivered a little and then jumped when she felt a coat being drape over her shoulders. She turned to find Andy standing behind her.

"What are you doing here?"

"Honestly, I was waiting for you to leave the bar." He stepped around the bench and sat next to her.

"You knew I was in the bar?"

"Cindy called and told me. I was watching from a table in the front corner."

She shook her head. "I thought you had a date with Lucy tonight?"

"Who?"

"Lucy, my friend that you met at the Purple Valley Tavern last night. Red hair, she was sitting with me."

"Oh, the lady who came joined me and the guys at the bar."

"That's her. Didn't you have a date with her tonight?"

"No. I think maybe Tom might have taken her out drinking though. He kind of liked her and she made it clear she was game for anything."

"Typical Lucy."

"Grace, I really want to talk tonight. Can we go somewhere?"

"I don't think that would be a good idea, Andy. I've drunk way too much to have a serious talk."

"But, Cindy said that you're leaving tomorrow and I have a feeling I won't have another chance."

He was right about that. "Let's just talk here."

"You're cold and I don't think my jacket is going to keep you warm with the falling temperatures. How about going to your room?"

"My room?" Even through her dizzy haze she knew that wasn't a good idea. "I don't think so."

"I promise, hands off and I'll be the perfect gentleman." He held his hands up in the air in front of him.

She didn't know if it was the tequila or the fact that she wouldn't see him again, but she gave in. "Okay, just talking. Nothing else."

"I promise."

She stood up, but wavered a little with Andy steadying her with his hand on her back. "I guess I had a little too much to drink tonight."

"We'll get some coffee once we get to the room," he suggested.

"Good idea."

They walked through the lobby and up the elevator to her room with Andy never taking his hand from her back.

She used her key card at the door and they went inside. "I need to use the restroom, can you start the coffee?"

"Sure."

She came out of the bathroom a few minutes later and found Andy sitting on the couch.

"Feeling better?"

"I didn't get sick, if that's what you mean. I just had to pee really bad."

"It's no wonder after all those margaritas I saw you drink tonight. As I recall, tequila was always your drink of choice, especially back when we shot them with salt and lime."

She looked at the coffee pot sitting empty, not even turned on. "Didn't you start the coffee?"

"I called room service for some and they said they would bring it right up. I thought I'd save what you have here in the room for your coffee in the morning."

She didn't want to sit on the bed, so she sat next to Andy on the couch.

"What time do you leave tomorrow?" he asked.

"We have a breakfast meeting at nine and the bus should be here around noon to take us all back."

"Did Cindy tell you about the class reunion?"

"Yes, but I'm not sure I'll be able to come. Work is usually pretty hectic and I take a lot of it home on the weekend to do."

Neither spoke for what seemed like minutes until there was a knock at the door. "Room service."

"I'll take care of this." Andy went to the door and let the server set a tray on the table. He handed him some money and the server left. Andy poured them each a cup of coffee and brought the tray over to the couch. "I thought you probably needed something to eat so I ordered a couple slices of pie. Chuck makes the best apple pie here at the hotel."

Grace took a bite and moaned. "You're right about that. It's delicious."

Andy sat down and they both devoured their food.

"I really needed that." She got up to put some sugar in her coffee. "It's getting late, you should say your peace and go." She sat back down on the couch.

He stood, took a deep breath, and began. "I understood that you had to go with your parents when you moved from here, but I still had plans for us. We would keep in touch and once I finished college and got a good job, I would propose to you and we'd come back here to marry and raise our kids. I didn't know at the time that I got things a little out of order."

"Go on."

"When you didn't answer any of my letters, I got upset and then worried. Then, Cindy said her mom heard from your mom about how things were going really great for you. That's when I got angry, even started hating you."

"You should hate me for what I did."

"No. I got past that. I grew up and knew one day I'd see you again and things would work out. I thought after our night at that cabin, I'd been right."

"But, then I dropped that bombshell on you."

"Yep, you sure did. I got all confused and angry all over again. After thinking long and hard over everything that's happened, I understand why you didn't tell me about the baby. You weren't selfish about it. You were thinking of me and my future."

"That's right."

"If you hadn't had that accident, would you have kept the baby?"

There it was, the question she'd been afraid he'd ask. "I'm not sure. I hadn't made that decision when the accident happened. I had mixed feelings about putting her up for adoption, but I would like to have thought I would have kept her."

"Her? It was girl?" He nearly had tears in his eyes.

"That's what they told me." Tears now streamed down her cheeks.

Andy walked over to the couch and reached for her hand, pulling her up into his arms. They both needed that.

Grace broke the embrace first. "You should probably get going and I need to get some sleep."

"Sure, you're right." They walked to the door. "Can we keep in touch this time?"

"Okay." She took a card off of the table and handed it to him. "Here's my card from work. You can email me there."

Before he went out the door, he pulled her into his arms again, this time for a kiss. He held her tight while his tongue parted her lips and swirled in circles inside her mouth. She suddenly felt herself kissing him back, while running her fingers through his hair.

He stepped back into the room, closing the door with is foot. He picked Grace up off the floor and carried her to the bed.

"Grace, I want you so badly. Please let me stay."

She shook her head yes and they both lay down on the bed together.

She unbuttoned his shirt and pitched it to the floor. Lying on his back, he removed his pants while she did the same with hers.

Before she could get her shirt unbuttoned, he caught her hand. "Leave some fun for me." He slowly unbuttoned the top button, revealing her skin. He planted a kiss after each button until he had worked all the way down to her stomach.

He moved his kisses back to her neck and rolled her over on top of him. With a quick flick of his finger, her bra was no longer an obstacle. She rose up straddling him as his hands found her plump swollen mounds.

Just as she remembered, his hands were calloused and rough from his work at the stables, and that sensation excited her all the more. He pulled her back down and rolled her onto her back.

Andy's hands were all over her from her neck down to her breasts, and finally between her legs.

Her head was telling her no, this was a bad idea, but her heart was overruling. He teased with tickles between her thighs. She felt her panties becoming wet and it wasn't long before he found that out as well. She raised her hips and he took the hint. With his forefinger, he slipped her panties down her legs and onto the floor.

He trailed his kisses up her leg until he reached her sweet spot. She spread her legs farther apart and when his mouth made contact, she shivered with excitement. "You like that, eh?"

She tried to restrain herself, but she felt out of control. She had her hands on his head as he explored farther into her.

"Oh my God! Andy, you have to take me now or I'm going to finish without you."

He moved on top of her and plunged his hard erection inside of her. She moaned when he felt him slide in. Their rhythm fell into sync right away and she felt her excitement growing and screamed at the climax.

"Gracie, I love you," he responded.

They slumped together in a pile on the bed, their sweaty sticky bodies still entwined. She felt his member still throbbing inside her as their breathing slowed to normal.

He rolled off her but pulled her next to him with his arm around her and her head lying on his chest. That was how they both fell asleep.

Chapter Five

The alarm clock woke Grace the next morning, and she sat up in bed with a start. The memories of the night before floated back into her head as she looked around and found herself alone. Could it have been a dream?

When she scooted to the edge of the bed and felt soreness, she knew it was no dream.

"Andy, are you in the bathroom?"

No answer.

Thank goodness he was not there, she thought as she grabbed some clean panties and bra and went to take a shower.

When she came out, she threw her clothes into her suitcase. "What was I thinking by sleeping with him again last night? I'm never going to drink that much again."

She really wasn't certain if she was mad because she slept with him, or because he wasn't there when she woke up.

After closing her suitcase, she looked around the room one more time, not so much for anything she left, but to make sure she hadn't missed a note from him. Finding nothing, she headed down to the lobby.

A concierge waited there to take luggage for her group to the bus while they went to their breakfast meeting. After he took her bag, she saw Silvia, Maria, and Lucy waiting for her.

"Good morning," Silvia said.

"Good morning. I need to turn my keycard back in. Why don't

you three go get a table and I'll be right in," Grace suggested.

"We'll see you inside," Maria said.

Grace scanned the lobby as she walked to the front desk. No Andy. She turned in her keycard to the clerk behind the counter, who then typed a few things on the computer. "Everything looks fine, Ms. Taylor. Your bill will be sent to your company. Thank you for staying with us."

"Can you check to see if I have any messages?"

The clerk typed again on the keyboard. "No, I don't see any messages for you."

"Thank you." Why was she feeling like this? She was glad this trip was over and she could get back to her own life and leave her past behind. She turned and ran into someone, nearly knocking them down. "Oh, I'm so sorry." She looked up and right into Andy's blue eyes.

"You didn't think I'd let you leave without seeing me again, did you?"

She started shaking her head. "Last night was another mistake. I drank too much and you knew it." She tried to move around him, but he stepped in front of her again.

"Give me five minutes, please."

"Five minutes. That's all."

He took her hand and they walked to a quiet corridor. "You may have drank a lot last night, but you knew exactly what you were doing. Just like you knew what you were doing when we were at that cabin. Gracie, you don't belong in the city. You belong here with me. We could have a long life together and have more babies. I want you to be my wife."

She refused to make eye contact with him. "Even if I wanted

to, I have a job. I can't just up and leave that. People depend on me."

"You can work here. I already talked to the guy who is going to manage that new ski resort. They're already hiring marketing people and when I told him about you, he said you sounded like the perfect person to head up their marketing department. The head of the marketing department, just like you said you wanted."

"Well, you seem to have it all worked out, don't you? Did you ever think that maybe you might want to ask me about working for them first?"

"I know you still love me. I could tell it at the cabin and I could tell it last night."

"Your five minutes are over."

"I'll be waiting for you across the street when your meeting's over," he said.

She pushed past him and into the meeting room.

* * * *

Around noon Andy and Cindy stood across the street from the hotel watching for Grace to come out. "There's not anything else you could have done, Andy. She knows how you feel. We just have to hope she feels the same way."

"I hope so. I never stopped loving her."

"I know." Cindy put her hand on his shoulder.

It wasn't long before a group of people starting filing out of the hotel. "That's her group," Cindy said.

Andy watched intently, waiting for Grace to come out. Finally, he saw her emerge from the hotel with her friends. She looked across the street at him and then turned her back to him talking to her friends. Just then, the bus pulled up in front of them for loading, blocking his view. He could see people walking on the bus taking their seats, but with the tinted windows he couldn't tell if Grace was one of them.

Looking as if everyone was finally seated, the door closed and the bus pulled away.

It seemed as though everything moved in slow motion. As the back part of the bus moved out of the way, he saw her. Grace stood in front of the hotel next to her suitcase. He couldn't believe it.

"Go, Andy!" Cindy exclaimed.

He ran across the street, nearly getting hit by a car, and into Grace's arms.

"I love you, Gracie," he whispered into her ear as they hugged.

THE END

ABOUT THE AUTHOR

Carol Preflatish lives in southern Indiana and shares a log cabin with her husband and two cats in what seems like an enchanted forest with a menagerie of wildlife constantly visiting. Her interest in writing began in high school when she worked as a reporter, photographer, and Sport's Editor for the school newspaper. She is currently the author of five novels and two non-fiction books. Carol enjoys writing romantic suspense and is a member of the Sisters in Crime organization and Kentuckiana Authors.

http://CarolPre.com
http://CarolPre.blogspot.com
http://www.facebook.com/AuthorCarolPreflatish